Books by Matt Christopher

Hard Drive to Short

HARD DRIVE
TO SHORT

by Matt Christopher

Illustrated by George Guzzi

LITTLE, BROWN AND COMPANY
BOSTON   TORONTO

LIBRARY OF CONGRESS CATALOG CARD NO. 69–10653

THIRD PRINTING

Published simultaneously in Canada
by Little, Brown & Company (Canada) Limited

PRINTED IN THE UNITED STATES OF AMERICA

To
Mary and Joe

Hard Drive to Short

1

THE Minuteman stepped into Dick Regan's pitch and smacked a grounder that headed for the hole between shortstop and second base. It looked as if it were going for a clean hit and the Minutemen fans roared.

Sandy Varga, playing deep short for the Spacemen, sprang into action. Sandy was short, but deceptively quick for a boy his size. He dashed toward second, speared the hop and whipped it to first.

"Out!" yelled the base umpire.

Three outs. The Spacemen trotted in, the Minutemen trotted out. It was the first ball game of the season. The bottom of the first inning was coming up.

Coach Mike Malone smiled. "Nice going, Sandy. You caught two tough grounders out there."

Sandy returned the smile. "Thanks, Coach."

"Pick up a bat, Sandy. You're third man up. Kerry Dean, you're leading off. Jules Anderson, you're batting second. Let's get that run back!"

The Minutemen were leading 1 to 0.

Kerry, a short, stocky redhead, played third base, threw right-handed and hit left-handed. Mark Davis, the Minutemen's southpaw pitcher, couldn't groove one over the plate and Kerry walked.

Mark was on the way to walking Jules

4

Anderson too. He pitched three balls, then rubbed the ball hard and wiggled his cap before he got ready to pitch again. His next two throws were strikes. His next was in there, too, and Jules blasted it down to third. The third baseman fumbled the hop and Jules was safely on first, Kerry on second.

"Lay it down, Sandy," ordered Coach Malone.

Sandy frowned. Lay it down? Why?

5

The coach knew he could hit. Why did he order a bunt? Sandy punched the top of his protective helmet and strode to the plate.

Mark Davis grooved the first pitch. Sandy shifted his feet, ran his right hand partway up the bat and let the ball hit the wood. The ball dribbled toward the pitcher. Sandy dropped the bat and bee-lined for first.

He was within two steps of the base when the first baseman stretched and caught the throw. "Out!" cried the ump.

Hiding his disgust, Sandy turned and headed back for the dugout. The bunt had advanced the runners to second and third, but he still wished he had been allowed to hit. He didn't like to bunt. How can you knock in runs by bunting?

Center fielder John "Oink" Decker

blasted a double between left and center fields, scoring Kerry and Jules. Then Marty Loomis, the Spacemen's catcher, struck out and Dick Regan flied out to left, ending the inning.

Sandy started out of the dugout, then rushed back to Duke Miller sitting on the bench, his ankles crossed. Duke was the Spacemen's alternate pitcher and was holding Sandy's wristwatch.

"Don't forget to let me know when it's twenty minutes to seven," reminded Sandy.

"I won't," Duke answered, then frowned. "What do you want to know that for?"

"I have to, that's why," replied Sandy.

"But suppose you're out on the field when it's twenty minutes of seven?" asked Duke in puzzlement. "What then?"

"Signal to me," said Sandy. "And don't forget. It's important."

The Minutemen began tagging Dick Regan's pitches and scored twice before Sandy snared a line drive for which he really had to jump. Later he ran behind Kerry and caught a high fly just inside fair territory for the second out, holding runners on second and third.

The next Minuteman doubled, scoring the two runs. Dick struck out the next man, but a lot of damage had been done. The Minutemen had scored four runs, going into the lead 5 to 2.

Right fielder Stubby Tobin, leading off for the Spacemen, grounded out on the second pitch. Nibbs Spry got on by luck. He hit a high fly to center and the fielder dropped it. First baseman Ken Bockman hit three fouls to the backstop screen, then flied out to third.

Leadoff man Kerry Dean was up again. He let two balls and a strike go by, then singled through short, advancing Nibbs to second base.

"Hit me in! Hit me in!" yelled Nibbs, who hollered more than anybody else on the team. But Jules Anderson, batting next, flied out to right and Kerry died on second.

Sandy started to rush out to short, then ran back to the dugout again. "Duke, what time is it now?" he asked, low enough so that no one else except Duke could hear him.

Duke looked at the watch. "Almost six-thirty."

"Wow!" muttered Sandy, and tore out

to short. "Let's get 'em, Dick! One, two, three!" He couldn't stay longer than twenty minutes of seven. Perhaps one minute longer. But that was *all*.

A hot grounder to second, directly at Nibbs. He reached down for it. The ball struck his glove, then glanced off to the outfield! An error!

Center fielder Oink Decker retrieved the ball and relayed it to Sandy, who had gone over to cover second. The runner stayed on first. Sandy quickly tossed it to Dick. "Let's go!" he yelled. "Let's get two!"

Doggone Nibbs. Why did he miss that grounder?

Crack! A blistering grounder between shortstop and second base. Sandy sped after it, dust spurting from his sneakers. He caught the ball in the pocket of his glove, rushed over and touched second, then pegged to first. In time by two steps!

A double play!

A Minuteman tripled. The next man hit a skyscraping fly to Oink and the top of the third inning was over. Even before Oink had caught the ball Sandy was running off the field. He hadn't much time left.

"Sandy! Oink! Marty!" Coach Malone named off the first three hitters. Sandy picked up his brown bat, slapped on his plastic helmet and hustled to the plate.

The first pitch came in, low and inside. Sandy swung. Missed!

"Make 'em be in there, Sandy!" yelled the coach.

Come on, Mark, Sandy pleaded silently. *Throw me a good one.*

As if Mark heard him the Minuteman pitcher threw one almost squarely over

11

the heart of the plate. Sandy swung. A line drive over short! He rounded first and stopped on second for a neat double.

Oink flied out. Marty Loomis smashed a grounder to short. The shortstop fumbled it and Marty was safe on first. Sandy stayed on second. Then Dick Regan laid into a high pitch and sent it over the left fielder's head for a clean triple, scoring Sandy and Marty.

Nibbs and some of the other guys patted Sandy happily on the back. "Nice hitting, Sandy." "You're playing like a million dollars."

Sandy grinned and went over to Duke. "How much more time?"

"One minute!"

Sandy took the watch from Duke and slipped it on his wrist. He waited long enough to see Stubby Tobin hit a hard

grounder to third. The third sacker missed it and Dick Regan scored. Sandy walked up to the coach.

"I have to leave, Coach," he said softly.

The coach stared at him. "Leave now? Why?"

Sandy shrugged. "I have to, that's all. It's important. I'll . . . I'll see you at the next game."

He picked up his glove and started running off toward the gate. "Hey, Sandy!" someone yelled. "Where are you going?"

Sandy didn't answer.

2

MOM was waiting for him in the back yard where she was watching Jo Ann playing with a large doll and Elizabeth with her dollhouse. Jo Ann was eighteen months old and Elizabeth five years old. That was why Sandy had to rush home. To take care of them. Pop worked overtime almost every night at a typewriter factory. He seldom got home before seven-thirty. And Mom had to start her evening job at the drugstore by then.

"I think you'd better leave a little sooner

the next time, Sandor," Mom said, pronouncing his name *Shandor,* as if it had an *h* in it. Mom and Pop had been born in Hungary and had come to the United States when their oldest child, Peter, was only a year old. That was seventeen years ago. "Mr. Browning would not like it if I arrived there late. Good-bye, dear. And watch your sisters."

" 'Bye, Mom," he said, and she hurried out of the yard. She had to walk to the drugstore. There weren't any buses in the small town of Sharil. And Pop had the car.

Sandy hadn't liked to break away in the middle of the ball game, especially since he had been playing so well for the team. But Jo Ann and Elizabeth were too young to be left alone even for a little while. Since Peter worked at a supermarket every weekday afternoon and evening, Sandy had to watch over the little ones.

He hoped Pop would get home sooner this evening. Then he could go back to the game. Of course he wouldn't play, but he'd see the rest of it.

He wondered how it was going, and felt rather proud about his own playing. He had caught four or five grounders and pop flies without an error, hit a sacrifice bunt and knocked out a double. That was pretty good for the first game of the season.

"Jo Ann, get back here. Don't you go through those bushes."

Jo Ann stopped in her tracks and turned her huge blue eyes on him. She was blond like Mom and her hair was long and curly.

"Rex," she said.

"You're not going over to see Rex," said Sandy gruffly.

He got off the steps where he had been sitting, twirling his baseball glove round and round on his wrist, and carried her back to near Elizabeth and the dollhouse. "Stay here," he commanded. "Play with Elizabeth."

He didn't trust Rex, the big shepherd dog the neighbors, the Traceys, owned. Rex was leashed to his doghouse and was allowed to run loose only when someone was with him.

Sandy didn't know why he didn't trust the dog. Maybe it was because Rex was so big. He wasn't sure. He just never had been close to Rex and didn't want his little sisters to get close to him, either.

At last a car drove into the driveway. Pop was home.

"Hi, children," he greeted them cheerfully. Jo Ann and Elizabeth ran to him and he stopped and kissed them. "And, you, Sandor. You are still in your baseball uniform. Did you play?" He pronounced Sandor like Mom did.

"Hi, Pop. I played three innings. Sacrificed and doubled."

Pop had seen Sandy play last year and the year before. Both he and Mom liked baseball and knew what almost every baseball term meant.

"Good," said Pop. "If you wish, you can go back to the ball game as soon as I wash up and change my clothes."

The girls went back to the dollhouse and Pop went into the house, carrying his dinner pail. He was a tall man. He had played soccer in Hungary and frequently went to see Sharil's high school soccer team play. He often said he wished he was young again and able to play. Sandy guessed that Pop must have been an excellent athlete.

Pop was in the house when a loud, familiar voice shouted from the street. "San . . . dy! Hey, San . . . dy!"

Sandy jumped off the porch steps and ran around to the front of the house. "Hi!" he said to his buddies, Nibbs Spry and Jules Anderson. "Who won?"

"We did," said Nibbs, grinning and showing a missing tooth. "Ten to nine. What a ball game!"

"The score was tied nine-all to the sixth inning," said Jules. "Then Punk Peters doubled and Cookie Lamarr knocked him in."

"For a while we thought the game was a goner," said Nibbs. "Ike Norman took your place at short and missed two easy grounders. That guy's no ballplayer. Why did you have to leave so soon, anyway? Duke said you didn't even want to tell Mr. Malone why you had to leave. Is it a secret?"

Before Sandy could answer, there was a shout from his father.

"Sandor!" his father's voice reached him from the other side of the house. "Where are you? Where is Jo Ann?"

Sandy whirled around. "Oh, gee . . . !" he blurted, and sprinted to the back yard. Elizabeth was playing near the dollhouse, but Jo Ann was nowhere in sight.

"Jo Ann! Jo Ann!" he yelled.

By sheer instinct he ran toward the shrubbery separating his house from the Traceys', and burst through to the other side.

"Jo Ann!" he yelled again. "Come back here!"

She was standing by Rex, the big shepherd dog, patting him on the head. "Big doggie," she was saying. "Big doggie."

3

REX perked up his ears and looked at Sandy. His curved, brown, white-tipped tail was still. Sandy had heard that a dog who didn't wag his tail wasn't friendly. Yet there was Jo Ann, patting Rex on the back, and Rex didn't seem to mind.

"Jo Ann! Get away from him!" Sandy ordered.

Jo Ann didn't move. "Big doggie," she repeated.

Rex wagged his tail and Sandy stepped

forward carefully. "Hi, Rex," he said. "Hi, boy."

He took Jo Ann's hand, then very gently reached over and patted Rex on the head. Rex peered curiously at him. His pink tongue was out and he was breathing fast. His tail wagged fast, too.

"I think he likes you two," said a voice from the house.

Sandy looked up, startled, and saw Mr. Tracey smoking a pipe and gazing at them through the screen door of the enclosed porch.

"Hi, Mr. Tracey. Jo Ann came here on her own and I'm taking her back."

"You won't have to worry about Rex," smiled Mr. Tracey. "He won't hurt her."

As Sandy led Jo Ann back through the shrubbery to their own back yard, relief washed over him. Now that he had been near Rex himself, he didn't need to be afraid of the big shepherd dog anymore. The Traceys had only had him about five or six weeks.

Just the same he wished there was a fence, besides the shrubbery, separating the two lots so that Jo Ann would not stray during those few seconds he took his eyes off her. It seemed that it was always *then* that she decided to take off for somewhere.

When he returned to the front of the house, Nibbs and Jules were busy playing catch. Luckily they had forgotten about asking again why Sandy had left the game early.

On Thursday the Spacemen tangled with the Ripcords and once again Sandy started at shortstop. The Spacemen had first raps and got their first run on a single by Sandy Varga with Kerry Dean on second base. Oink Decker walked and then Marty Loomis blasted a double, scoring Sandy and giving the Spacemen two runs that first inning.

They led till the bottom of the third, when a Ripcord popped a fly high up into the air that started dropping in short left center field. Left fielder Jules Anderson, center fielder Oink Decker and shortstop Sandy Varga all ran after it and yelled, "I've got it!" at the same time.

Then each player, thinking that the others would catch it, stepped away from the ball — and it dropped between them!

The three boys stared at one another. Then Sandy broke from the shock that momentarily had gripped him, picked up the

ball and looked to see where the runners
were, for the Ripcords had two men on
base before this last hit. One runner had
scored and the second was rounding third.

Sandy pegged the ball home. The Ripcords' third-base coach yelled at the runner and got him back to third. One run had scored on that blunder.

I should have taken it, thought Sandy. But I was sure that either Jules or Oink was going to . . .

The Ripcords scored once more that inning, then Sandy made a neat catch on a grass-skimming grounder and pegged to first to keep the Ripcords from scoring more runs.

"Nice play, Sandy," Coach Malone said. Then he shook his head, disgusted. "Boys, listen. On that fly ball in the outfield . . . I've warned you guys a dozen times about a play like that. When three of you are able to catch a pop fly, *let the fielder coming in after the ball catch it. Yell for him to take it.* It isn't that hard!"

He smiled and squeezed Sandy and Jules on the shoulder. "Forget it this time. Just do it right the next time. Once in a while even the pros make that same mistake."

Sandy was able to bat only once more before twenty minutes to seven rolled around and he had to leave. He got his second hit, a three-bagger, scoring Ken Bockman. Oink popped up to end the top of the half-inning. The score was 3 to 2 in the Spacemen's favor. Two of those runs had been knocked in by Sandy.

"You're playing great ball, Sandy," the coach said to him as he started to leave. "You're a natural."

Sandy smiled. "Thanks, sir. I've got to go now."

"We won't be playing again until next

Thursday," said Coach Malone. "So be here Tuesday at five o'clock for practice. Okay?"

"Okay!" said Sandy, and started running off the field.

"Hey, Sandy!" a guy yelled at him. "Where are you going?"

Sandy didn't tell him. The guys might make fun of him if he told them he had to babysit with his little sisters. They didn't have to know.

He was walking by a large white house when he saw Rod Temple in the driveway, sitting on his bright red motor scooter, trying to start it. Rod was in high school and played second base with the Redwings, Sharil's town team. But Rod was no ordinary second baseman. He was the best, and very popular.

"Hi, Rod," greeted Sandy.

"Well hi, kid. Been playing ball?"

"Yeah." He didn't want to say anymore about the game, not unless Rod asked him specific questions. He didn't want to tell Rod he had to go home to watch his sisters. Even Rod might laugh about that.

"Saw in the paper you play pretty good ball. Keep that up and someday you'll be playing with the Redwings."

Sandy grinned, but he didn't know what to say.

"Want to take a spin?" Rod asked. "Around a few blocks, maybe?"

Sandy's eyes popped. "A ride? On your motor scooter?"

"Sure!" Rod grinned. "Come on. Climb on the back seat."

Sandy wanted to very much. It wasn't

only the ride on the motor scooter he'd enjoy. It was being with Rod.

"Thanks, Rod. But I've got to get home."

Rod chuckled. "What's the matter? Scared?"

Sandy's face reddened. "No, I'm not scared. I'll take a ride some other time. I promise!"

Rod's laughter drifted after Sandy as he ran across the street and into his own driveway. He couldn't get over it. Rod, a great second baseman, a guy a lot of kids would give a dollar to be with, had asked Sandy to go riding with him!

Mom left a few seconds after Sandy got home. Jo Ann and Elizabeth were in the back yard, playing with the dollhouse.

"Who won the game?" Elizabeth asked, putting diapers on her doll.

"Nobody yet," answered Sandy. "It's only half over." *I wish you and Jo Ann were bigger*, he thought. *Then I wouldn't have to babysit. I could be with Rod Temple on his motor scooter.* But he wouldn't be, he suddenly realized. He'd still be at the game.

Anyway, he liked Rod Temple and Rod liked him. They were two of a kind, thought Sandy. It made no difference that Rod was older and bigger than he. They *both* could do something extra good. They both were real good ballplayers. Everyone knew that Rod Temple was the best player on the Redwings. And Coach Malone had practically said that Sandy was the best player with the Spacemen.

Later Nibbs and Jules stopped in and told him that the Spacemen had won the game 6 to 4. Pop was home by now and Sandy had changed into his everyday clothes. They had supper which Mom had prepared and left in the oven.

The house seemed empty without Mom and Peter at the table. Especially without Mom. She had said she would work for a year. By that time the combined savings of Mom, Pop, and Peter would be enough to put Peter through his first year of college and give him a good start toward his second year. Mom might have to work again after that. It all depended.

Sandy was looking at his model of a missile capsule — it was eighteen inches long with two astronauts strapped inside of it — and thinking about Rod Temple. In a little while he might see if Rod was in the driveway with his motor scooter. Perhaps Rod might offer him a ride again.

Someone knocked on the front door. Sandy heard Pop answer it, then Pop's raised voice. "Sandy! Nibbs and Jules are here to see you!"

"Okay, Pop!" He ran out of his room and met them at the door.

"Hi, Sandy." Nibbs Spry's hair was still wet from a shower. "We're going to play miniature golf. Want to come along?"

Sandy looked at them, unable to make up his mind. He enjoyed playing miniature golf with the guys, but what if Rod was out there? What if this might be his chance to ride on Rod's motor scooter? He could play miniature golf any time.

"I — I'm busy, guys," he said lamely. "Maybe next time. Okay?"

The two boys looked at him. "Okay,"

said Nibbs, his smile fading. He and Jules walked away and Sandy closed the door.

Later on he wished he had gone with Nibbs and Jules because he didn't see Rod and his motor scooter that evening at all.

4

ON Saturday afternoon Rod Temple was polishing his motor scooter again and Sandy walked across the street to watch him.

"Hi, Rod," he greeted.

"Hi, Sandy. Polishing up this baby again. You'd be surprised how quick she gets dirty."

Sandy didn't think that the motor scooter ever got as dirty as Rod implied. It always looked as clean and new as the day Rod had purchased it. Like now. You could see your reflection in it even if the curves distorted it.

"Got time?" asked Rod. "I'll take you for a ride."

Sandy was elated. His wish was answered. "Okay." He didn't want to sound as excited as he felt.

Rod stood away from the scooter and looked at it. "Well, the shine's still not too good but I won't spend more time with it now. Let's take our ride."

He stuck the chamois cloth into a leather pouch behind the front seat, then turned the scooter around so that it faced the street. He got on and Sandy climbed on behind him.

Rod started the motor and carefully drove out of the driveway, then sped down the street. The motor put-putted loudly as the little scooter, weaving slightly from left to right for a few seconds, evened its course and shot straight ahead. Sandy hung on tight to the handgrips of his seat, the wind lashing his hair and caressing his cheeks. What fun this was! It was the first time he had ever ridden on a motor scooter.

They rode down the street for several blocks, then turned left. Sandy wasn't thinking about where they were going. He was thinking only of the ride and of being with Rod.

"Hi, Sandy!" a voice suddenly shouted. Two others joined in.

Oink Decker, Marty Loomis and Ken Bockman were waving to him from the sidewalk. He took a hand off the grip and waved back. He wondered if they envied him. Well, let them. He deserved to ride with Rodney.

The scooter pulled up to a curb in front of an ice cream store. "How about an ice cream cone?" asked Rod, digging into his pocket.

"Okay."

After a few moments of searching Rod said, "Oh-oh. Left all my dough at home."

"I've got plenty," Sandy piped up enthusiastically. "I'll buy."

"You sure it's okay?"

"Sure, I'm sure." Sandy lifted out his wallet. "What kind do you like?"

"Maple walnut."

"I'll get two. Double headers?"

Rod grinned. "Double headers!"

Sandy bought them while Rod stood outside with his scooter. They ate the ice cream, then started up the scooter and rode on. They arrived at Fillmore Park, a huge, beautiful place with two ball diamonds, tennis courts and picnic grounds in the wooded hills beyond. A high waterfall sparkled gorgeously to the left. Below, in a dammed-up pond, people were diving and swimming.

A game was in progress on one of the ball diamonds.

"Hey," said Rod, suddenly smiling, "the girls are playing softball! I know some of them. Let's watch them for a while."

Watch girls play softball? Was Rod kidding? For a minute Sandy thought that Rod really was. But Rod was already walking toward them, a broad, happy smile on his face.

"Can I finish polishing the scooter while you're watching the game?" asked Sandy. That would be more fun than watching girls play softball.

"Oh, sure. Go ahead."

"Thanks, Rod!"

Sandy got the chamois cloth out of the pouch and went to work on the scooter. He could not see where it really needed polishing but he rubbed and rubbed all over the bright metal surface anyway. Now and then he looked up, hoping that Rod would return so they could be on their way.

But Rod seemed to have made himself comfortable on the grass next to one of the girls' team's benches. Sandy put the cloth away, sat and waited. Rod didn't leave until the game was over. By that time Sandy was really tired of hanging around.

He said nothing, though. Guess when guys got older they hung around with girls some. Sandy didn't care. He felt good just being with Rod. Not only good, but big, too.

5

THE next time Sandy saw Rodney was early Tuesday afternoon. Rodney took him riding on the motor scooter again and stopped at a miniature golf course at the edge of town.

"How about playing a game?" Rod asked.

"Okay. But you'll beat me. I'm not good at miniature golf."

"So what?" They got off the scooter and Rod pulled it back on its stand. Then he reached into his pocket. Suddenly a look

Sandy had seen on Rod's face before was there again.

"Well," said Rod, "guess we don't play. Stupid me. I forgot my wallet again."

Once more Sandy brought out his wallet.

"Forget it," said Rod. "We can play some other time."

"I've got money for both of us," insisted Sandy. "I'll pay."

Rod grinned. "Boy, it seems that you're always loaded. How do you make your money, kid?"

Sandy shrugged. "I get an allowance every week for doing chores around the house and watching my sisters. My mother works, too."

"Oh, no wonder!" Rod's grin widened. "In that case, I'll let you pay! But you'll have to let me pay sometime. Okay?"

"Okay." The way Rod looked at him, the way he said that — Sandy didn't know whether Rod was kidding him, or what.

They played golf and Rod won by four points.

An hour before the Batwings–Spacemen game on Thursday, Sandy, dressed in his baseball uniform and carrying his glove on his wrist, walked across the street to see if Rod was out on the driveway. He wasn't. Neither was the scooter, though it could be in the garage.

Sandy had hoped he'd see Rod. Maybe, just maybe, Rod might have offered to give him a ride to the game.

Disappointed, Sandy walked the four blocks to the ball field.

"You're not going to be running home halfway through the game today, are you?" Marty Loomis said as they played catch with each other.

"I've got to be home by a quarter of seven," replied Sandy.

"Why?"

"I have something to do, that's why. Now quit asking questions, will you?"

You couldn't tell every guy on the team you had to watch over your little sisters. They'd razz you to the ground.

The Batwings had first raps. Sandy started at short. Duke Miller was on the mound.

"All right! Some noise out there!" yelled Coach Malone from the bench. "What are you — statues?"

The men started chattering like a cage full of monkeys. The Batwings' leadoff man stepped to the plate. Duke, a left-hander, stepped to the mound. Catcher Marty Loomis gave him a sign. Duke wound up and delivered. The batter swung at the first pitch. *Crack!* A sizzling grounder to short.

For an instant Sandy felt his nerves jangle. He had thought he was ready for a ball hit toward him, but now that it was coming at him he felt caught off guard. The batter's hitting that first pitch was a surprise.

"Take it, Sandy!" shouted Kerry Dean from third.

Sandy bent over to field the ball. It was coming hard and fast, faster than he realized. He lowered his glove, felt the ball smack solidly into the pocket, then rose and pegged it to first.

Out!

"Nice play, Sandy!" Nibbs Spry yelled from the other side of the keystone sack.

The ball zipped around the horn. Sandy caught the throw from Kerry, tossed it to Nibbs, then stood in his position at short, swinging his arms loosely back and forth in front of him. Man! he thought, was he lucky. He had expected to miss that grounder for sure.

The Batwings' second batter came to the plate. Duke threw three pitches before the batter took his first cut. He missed, then cracked a line drive over the third-base sack that went for two bases.

The next hitter, a lefty, banged an inside pitch to right field, scoring the man from second. Stubby Tobin's throw-in held the hitter on first.

The Batwings' clean-up hitter fouled off two pitches, then socked a high-bouncing

ground ball to Sandy. Sandy fielded it, snapped it to Nibbs. Nibbs stepped on second, pegged the ball to first. A double play!

Sandy smiled. He felt better.

First at bat for the Spacemen was Kerry Dean, who waited out the pitcher, taking two balls and two strikes before his first cut. It was a strikeout.

Jules Anderson let a strike go by him, then laced the next pitch just inside the first-base bag for a double. He stood on the sack, clapping his hands and yelling for Sandy to knock him in. Sandy stepped to the plate. The guys on the bench and the fans began yelling, too.

"Bring 'im in, Sandy! Bring 'im in!"

His face was hot. His palms sweated. He wiped them on his pants, then gripped his bat close to the knob and waited for Ed Thomas, the Batwings' pitcher, to put one in there.

In it came, chest-high. Sandy swung. Missed! "Strike!" said the ump.

Another. "Strike two!"

Sandy stepped out of the box, dried his hands on his pants, then stepped in again.

6

"BALL!"

The first nervous sensations were gone. Sandy felt more sure of himself. Ed had speed, but his curve was just a wrinkle.

The pitch came in. It was knee-high and curving. Sandy cut at it. *Crack!* The ball struck the ground in front of Ed, bounced over his head and to the outfield. Frank Mintz, coaching at third, windmilled Jules on to home. The throw-in from the outfield held Sandy on first.

Well, he had done it. He had evened the score.

Oink Decker blasted a hot grounder to shortstop and Sandy ran as hard as he could to second, not thinking he'd ever make it. The shortstop fumbled the ball! By the time he retrieved it the men were safe on their bases.

Marty Loomis connected solidly with the first pitch, but it was a high fly to right field and easily caught. Two away.

Stubby Tobin was up next. He waited out the pitcher till there was a three-two count on him, then smashed a line drive over short. The ball hit the grass behind the bare ground and rolled out between the left and center fielders. Sandy scored from second. A quick retrieve and throw-in from the center fielder held Oink up at third.

Nibbs Spry, looking anxious and dangerous at the plate, did no more than foul two pitches to the backstop screen. He struck out, ending the first inning.

Sandy felt good as he ran out to short and picked up his glove. Two to one. If only the Spacemen could pick up a few more runs before he had to leave.

He was prepared this time for a first-pitch hit. But the leadoff man took it. "Strike one!" called the umpire.

Duke laid the next pitch in there, too. The batter swung. The blow was solid, driving the ball like a meteor to deep right field. It hit behind Stubby. Before Stubby picked it up and pegged it in, the runner was on third base.

The next batter hit a high-bouncing grounder to second base. The runner on third took off the instant the ball was hit.

Nibbs fielded it and whipped it home. The peg was a mile high over Marty's head and every Spacemen fan in the stands groaned. So did Nibbs. The runner scored and the hitter ran to second.

A scratch single advanced the man to third. Duke was on his way to walking the next hitter. He threw three balls without a strike. Then he shot two straight over the heart of the plate.

"Atta boy, Duke!" yelled Sandy. "Groove the next one in there, too!"

"Belt it out of the county, Nick!" a Batwing fan shouted.

Duke pitched. *Crack!* A high, towering fly over the infield!

"I'll take it! I'll take it!" called Sandy.

The ball became a fuzzy white sphere against the velvet blue sky, and Sandy was afraid he might misjudge it. Then it came down. *Step back! Step back! It's coming down behind you!* He raised his glove. *Plop!* He had it.

Duke smiled as Sandy tossed him the ball. "It was an infield out, anyway," said Duke.

"Yes, but those guys could've run if the ball wasn't caught," reminded Sandy.

A blazing grounder through the pitcher's mound scored the Batwings' second run, and again left men on first and third. The infielders talked it up loud and steadily, hoping to give Duke the encouragement he needed to pitch well to the next batter.

He threw a strike. The next ball was hit to short right field. Stubby Tobin ran in as hard as his short legs would carry him. He dove at the ball, and missed it, landing on his stomach. He clambered to his feet, chased after the ball, snapped it up and

pegged it in, holding the runner on third.

But another run had scored, making it three so far this inning. And there were men on second and third.

Why in heck had Stubby run in after that ball, anyway? thought Sandy angrily. He ought to know he wasn't *that* fast.

Duke pitched to the following batter, getting two balls and a strike on him. Then, a hot, eight-foot-high drive to Sandy! The ball was curving downward slightly as it headed for him. He leaped, snagged it. He saw the runner on third returning to tag up. Sandy snapped the ball to Kerry. Out! A double play!

Coach Malone smacked the shortstop on the seat of the pants as he came in to sit down. "Nice catch and quick thinking, buddy."

"Thanks," replied Sandy, taking a deep breath.

He hoped his teammates would rally and get back those three runs. The Batwings led, 4 to 2. But his hopes vanished as Duke hit into a double play with Ken Bockman on first. Kerry singled. Jules flied out.

Sandy checked the time with Phil Peters, who was holding his wristwatch. Phil was the Spacemen's mascot and Punk Peters's kid brother. It was ten after six. He had half an hour to play before he had to leave.

The top of the third. Duke looked hot as he mowed down the first batter with three called strikes. The second batter lined a sizzling grounder to Nibbs. Nibbs fumbled it, picked it up quickly and pegged to first. A close play.

"Out!" yelled the base umpire.

Good ol' Nibbs, Sandy reflected. The best second baseman in the league.

Duke walked the third batter, but the fourth popped a fly to him, ending the half-inning.

Sandy Varga led off, and the Spacemen fans began yelling for him again. He thought of Rod Temple, wondering if Rod was in the stands. But Rod was probably practicing baseball, or playing in a game himself.

Crack! A smashing drive between left and center fields! Sandy dropped his bat and ran. He rounded first . . . second. Frank Mintz, coaching third, held him up at the third-base sack.

Well, he had started it off. *Let's keep it going, guys! Don't let me die here!*

Oink Decker answered Sandy's wish. He belted a single, scoring Sandy. Marty walked. Then Stubby got a free pass, filling the bases. Nibbs smacked a grounder to second, and it looked as if it were going to be a double killing for sure. But the second baseman muffed the ball and couldn't retrieve it in time to throw anyone out. Oink scored.

The Spacemen bench was wild with excitement. Now they had the game going like a roller coaster.

Ken Bockman went down swinging for the first out. Then Duke Miller hit a slow grounder to short. All the runners took off. Marty scored. The shortstop fielded the ball and made the play to second, throwing out Nibbs. With Stubby on third and Duke on first, leadoff man Kerry Dean singled, bringing in the fourth run of the inning. Jules belted the first pitch out to deep right, but it was caught. Three outs. But the fat inning put the Spacemen into the lead, 6 to 4.

It was nearly six-thirty. Sandy became anxious as one by one the Batwings belted Duke for safe hits. A run scored. Then another and the score was tied!

It must be twenty minutes of seven now, thought Sandy worriedly. It must be. A hard grounder sizzled down to him. He reached for it, missed it. Another run scored.

"Time!" yelled Coach Malone. "Sandy, come on out!"

Impatience was written all over Mom's face as Sandy pounded into the house. He waited anxiously for almost an hour for Nibbs Spry and Jules Anderson to come by. They told him that the Spacemen had won, 11 to 8.

7

ON Saturday morning Mom sent Sandy to the store to purchase two dozen eggs. She had forgotten to include them on the list of groceries she had purchased Friday morning. Sandy crossed the tree-shadowed street so that he would walk by Rod Temple's house. He hadn't seen Rod in three days.

Rod was in the driveway, working on the motor scooter.

"Hi, Rod," he greeted, stopping at the edge of the sidewalk.

"Hi, Sandy. Where are you going so early in the morning?"

"Got to buy eggs," replied Sandy.

Rod said the gas line had sprung a leak and he was fixing it. The sound of loud voices came from the house and Sandy thought it must be Rod's mother and father. He looked toward an open screened window from where the full volume of the voices seemed to come, then he turned quickly away with embarrassment. Mr. and Mrs. Temple were arguing fiercely.

Rod grinned at Sandy and shrugged his shoulders. "They're at it again this morning. My old man came home plastered to the gills last night and he doesn't want to go to work this morning, so Mom is giving it to him."

The argument kept on. And the longer

Sandy stayed the more uncomfortable he felt.

"I wish they'd cut it out," grumbled Rod.

Sandy started to leave. "See you, Rod," he said. "I've got to go."

"Sure," said Rod.

Sandy was glad to get away from there. What a miserable household to live in! It seemed to bother Rod, too. Maybe more than he showed.

Sandy purchased the eggs and returned home. About half past one Nibbs Spry, Jules Anderson and some other guys came to the house. They were carrying their swimming trunks. The sun had risen high, the sky was clear, and the temperature had soared to ninety-six degrees.

"Come on swimming with us," Nibbs

invited. "Let's get out of this heat for a while."

Sandy stood on the threshold of the front door, feeling the heat envelop him. The cool pool was indeed the place to be in now. He was about to tell him to wait while he got his trunks when he spotted Rod Temple coming out of his house and heading for the garage.

"Ah . . . no, thanks," replied Sandy, cracking a weak smile. "You guys go, yourselves."

Jules frowned and looked over his shoulder. Rod was opening the garage door.

"Oh, I see," he said. "You're going with Rod Temple on his motor scooter."

Sandy shrugged. "I might."

Ike Norman yanked Nibbs's sleeve. "Come on. Let's go."

Punk Peters was already on his way. "Come on, guys," he said curtly. "I can't hang around all day."

The others turned and followed him. Sandy hopped off the porch and ran across the street. Just as he reached the garage Rod came out and closed the door. He had a couple of wrenches in his hand.

"Hi, Sandy," he greeted. "What's new?"

Sandy's smile faded. "Fixing something, Rod?"

"Not me. My father is. The kitchen sink sprung a leak."

"Oh. Well . . . see you again, Rod."

"Sure thing, kid."

Sandy went back across the street and looked for the guys. They were out of sight. Well, heck, he didn't feel like going swimming now, anyway.

8

THE Spacemen had first raps in their game against the Sharks on Tuesday, June 21. Red Billings, the Sharks' tall right-hander, got easily by Kerry Dean and Jules Anderson. Kerry flied out to short and Jules fanned. Then Sandy stepped to the plate.

Sandy knew that Red had a pitch that curved in toward a right-hand hitter. A lot of batters were hitting that in-curve near the handle of their bats, knocking the ball weakly to the infield or popping it up. Sandy stepped a few inches farther back

69

from the plate, dug his sneakers into the dirt and waited for Red's first pitch.

"Ball!" shouted the ump.

Sandy tapped the bat against the plate and got set again.

"Ball two!"

Then Red placed one down the center of the plate. "Steeerike!"

"Wallop it out of the park, Sandy!" cried a fan.

Red's arm came over and the ball whistled in toward the outside corner of the plate. Sandy started to swing. Held up.

"Strike two!"

Sandy stepped back and looked at the umpire. The umpire smiled at him. "That was in there, Sandy," he said.

Sandy didn't argue with him. He stepped back into the box, tugged on his helmet, held his bat high. In came the pitch, letter-high, slightly close. Sandy swung. A smashing drive to deep left center field!

Sandy rounded first, second and was held up at third by third-base coach Punk Peters. "Nice hit, Sandy," said Punk.

Oink Decker cracked out a single through the pitcher's box and Sandy scored. Marty Loomis got a lucky break when the shortstop missed his grounder. Dick Regan was lucky, too. The right fielder missed his high fly, advancing Oink to third and Marty to second, filling the bases.

"A grand slammer, Stubby!" yelled the Spacemen fans. "Now's your chance, boy!"

Red Billings was sweating. He took off his cap and wiped his face with the sleeve of his jersey. Then he looked around at the men on bases and finally at Stubby Tobin.

Stubby was short and stout and didn't look dangerous at all. As a matter of fact he looked scared facing tall Red Billings.

Red pitched. "Strike!" yelled the ump.

"Come on, Stubby! Come on, boy!" cried the men on the bench. "Show 'em you can do it!"

"Strike two!" the ump yelled again.

"Red's going to mow him down one, two, three," muttered Kerry Dean.

Red delivered. The ball smoked in. And Stubby swung. *Crack!* The ball shot like a white meteor toward left field and every head in the stands turned. Every pair of eyes seemed to pop. The ball sailed over the fence for a home run!

"He did it!" yelled Nibbs, jumping to his feet in the on-deck circle. "Stubby did it! He blasted a grand slammer!"

You never saw a happier guy than

Stubby Tobin as he trotted around the bases and into the dugout, where Coach Malone and every member of the team shook his hand. It was the first home run of his career.

"Keep it going, Nibbs!" someone yelled. But Nibbs flied out, ending the top half of the first inning.

Five runs, thought Sandy, as he hustled out to short. That wasn't a bad start.

Lucky Stubby. Sandy was glad for him. Stubby was a nice kid.

Dick Regan, pitching for the Spacemen, struck out the first Shark. The next socked a hard grounder to first baseman Ken Bockman. The ball struck Ken on a toe of his right foot and glanced out to the outfield.

"Get two!" yelled Sandy.

But it was the Sharks who got two. Two runs. The next hitter blasted Dick's third pitch over the left field fence.

The two runs seemed to perk up the Sharks' confidence. They knocked out another single. Then Sandy leaped for a line drive that streaked like a bullet over his head. He caught it one-handed, whipped it to first. The runner didn't get back in time to tag up. A double play!

"Terrific play, Sandy," said the coach as

Sandy trotted in. "You robbed that guy of a hit."

Sandy grinned. "He hit it hard, too. It really stung."

Ken Bockman led off the top of the second and flied out to center. Leadoff man Kerry Dean singled through short, then was put out on a double play on Jules's grounder to the second baseman.

The Sharks picked up a run, giving them three to the Spacemen's five. But the Spacemen had a field day again in the top of the third. Sandy, first up, singled over short. The third baseman fumbled Oink's grounder, advancing Sandy to second. Then Marty struck out and Dick popped out to the pitcher. It looked as if that might be it for the Spacemen. But Stubby Tobin came through again, this time with a single, scoring Sandy. Nibbs kept the rally alive by blasting a drive down to third which the third baseman also missed, scoring Oink.

Then Ken Bockman came to the plate, tall and skinny as a beanpole, and drilled Red Billings's first pitch to right center field for a clean triple. Kerry, up again, struck out, ending the half-inning. The Spacemen had scored four runs.

Sandy looked at his wristwatch. He was wearing it now. He wasn't going to ask anyone to hold it while he played. It was six-thirty-five.

"Coach," he said, "I have to leave in five minutes. You want to put someone in my place now?"

Coach Malone looked at him. "Sandy, why do you have to leave every game just about the same time?"

Sandy's neck turned scarlet. "I — I have

to watch my little sisters," he confessed. "My father works late and my mother has to leave for work at a quarter of seven. But, please — please don't tell the guys. They'd razz me."

Coach Malone grinned. "So that's it. Well, okay. Go right now if you want to."

Sandy didn't, though. He stayed till the last minute. The Sharks didn't score in the bottom of the third. It was exactly six-forty when Sandy sprinted for home.

"Hey, look!" Ike Norman shouted. "There he goes again!"

"And the game's only half over!" said Marty Loomis.

"How do you like that?" said Stubby. "And he leaves without saying a word to us!"

Sandy ignored the remarks.

He read the results of the game in the

paper the next day. The Spacemen had beat the Sharks 12 to 6 with "spectacular hitting by Sandy Varga, Stubby Tobin and Ken Bockman for the Spacemen, and Ron Halsey for the Sharks. Tobin had a grand slammer and Halsey a homer with one on. Varga turned in some sparkling plays at shortstop for the Spacemen," the article added.

Sandy wondered if Rod would see that.

On Thursday the Spacemen played the Minutemen. The two times that Sandy was up to bat he flied out to center and tripled, scoring a run. In the third inning he fumbled a hard hit grounder that resulted in a run for the Minutemen. He wished he could play longer to make up for it, but he couldn't. Six-forty came and he had to leave. The Spacemen were leading 4 to 2.

He stayed in the back yard with Elizabeth and Jo Ann, hoping the guys would drop in after the game and tell him how it had turned out.

Pop was already home when Sandy saw Nibbs, Jules, Punk and Ike walking by. He stared at them from the yard. They could see him easily if they looked. But they were *across* the street, and always before they had walked on this side of it.

And not one of them looked toward him. Not one.

9

SANDY VARGA read the results of the Spacemen–Minutemen game in Friday's Sharil *Journal*. What a surprise. When he had left the game the Spacemen had been leading 4 to 2. It had ended 6 to 5, the Minutemen winning!

The box score:

	AB	R	H		AB	R	H
Dean 3b	4	1	0	Loomis c	4	0	0
Anderson lf	1	2	1	Miller p	3	0	1
bLamarr	2	0	0	Tobin rf	2	0	1
Varga ss	2	1	1	Spry 2b	3	0	0
cMintz	2	0	0	Bockman 1b	1	0	0
Decker cf	2	0	1	aNorman	1	1	1
dPeters	2	0	1	Totals	29	5	7

a–Walked for Bockman in 4th.
b–Flied out for Anderson in 4th.
c–Struck out for Varga in 5th.
d–On base by error for Decker in 5th.

| Spacemen | 103 | 001–5 |
| Minutemen | 020 | 220–6 |

Frankie Mintz, who had replaced Sandy at short, had not gotten a hit. Neither had Kerry Dean, Marty Loomis or Nibbs Spry, all of whom had played the entire game. Mark Davis, the Minutemen's skinny, left-handed pitcher, wasn't *that* good. But, then, maybe he was.

Well, at least the score was close. And it was the first game the Spacemen had lost.

After lunch Mom asked Sandy and Peter to carry the vacuum cleaner into the basement and clean it up.

"The spider webs, too," she said. "They are making the cellar look like an old deserted house. We are here, aren't we? Let us make the spiders know that."

Sandy chuckled. He didn't mind spiders. He found them interesting creatures after reading how they wove their webs and how cunning they were in capturing flies and moths. He had a collection of them once — all large — and had to throw them away when Pop found out about it. Pop had no stomach for spiders.

Peter left at a quarter of one to be at the supermarket by one o'clock. Sandy grumbled about doing the rest of the work by himself, but remembered that Peter *had* to work to help pay for his way through college. He was hoping he could make the freshmen basketball team in college.

Sandy finished the job, put the vacuum cleaner back into the closet and went outdoors. Just as the screen door slammed shut behind him, he heard Elizabeth shout, "Jo Ann! Come back here! I *told* you!"

Sandy saw his little sister next door, crouched beside Rex, petting him, while the big shepherd lay there, resting his long jaws on his forepaws. Sandy shook his head and wondered how long she had been there.

Well, there was no need to fear Rex. But Sandy went over and got Jo Ann anyway, and told her that her place was here, not there.

As he walked back with her, Sandy glanced between the two houses toward the Temples' and saw Rod in the driveway, checking the gas in the motor scooter. Rod was wearing his Redwings baseball uniform.

"Hi, Rod!" Sandy yelled over.

Rod turned and waved. "Hi! Hey, Sandy, want to come along?"

"To the ball game?"

"Yeah!"

Sandy beamed. "Wait a second! I'll see!"

He rushed into the house and asked Mom if he could go. He was all excited. It was the first time Rod had asked him to go with him to a Redwings ball game.

She gave him permission, and also a dollar he asked for, promising he'd "work it off the next two weeks."

"Just make sure you are home by half past six," reminded Mom.

"Oh, sure, Mom!"

He ran over to Rod's as Rod started the motor scooter, and hopped on the rear seat. Seconds later they were buzzing down the street, the motor cracking and spitting before it settled down to a loud, even roar.

The roar softened as the scooter made a left turn at the next block, hopped over a little hump in the street, picked up speed again. This was the life, thought Sandy. Here was a brand-new world of fun and excitement.

Presently, ahead of them, Sandy saw Nibbs Spry, Jules Anderson and Punk Peters walking on the sidewalk. Sandy turned his head. They would just think that he hadn't seen them.

10

THE scooter breezed along the black ribbon of highway that ran alongside Deerhead Lake, a glossy, flat mirror of water that stretched out for miles ahead of them. Five miles farther on they crossed a steel bridge. The water underneath flowed from a hundred-foot-high falls that was hidden beyond the curve of the gorge cut out by glaciers millions of years ago and emptied into the lake.

A quarter of a mile past the bridge a road turned off from the main highway and up a steep hill. Rod swung onto it, and the motor scooter slowed down almost instantly. Higher and higher they climbed, and farther and farther away from the lake. Soon dense trees separated them from it, and the lower road could no longer be seen.

Many times Mom and Pop had driven the children along that lower road, absorbing the beautiful scenery. They said that the view reminded them of parts of Hungary.

Sandy hadn't realized that this road was also a shortcut to the next town where the Redwings were playing today. They reached the baseball park five minutes before the game started. The Rock Salts, the team the Redwings were playing, were already having their final infield practice.

"Where've you been?" the manager snapped at Rod as he trotted to the dugout. "We're almost ready to go."

Sandy didn't hear Rod's answer. He walked behind the backstop screen, looking for a seat in the crowded stands. He found one halfway up and sat down.

The Redwings had first raps and Rod was third man up. The leadoff man struck out and the second batter walked. Then Rod stepped to the plate.

"Come on, Rod! Drill it out of the lot!"

You could tell that Rod had a lot of fans by the way they shouted for him. Sandy felt lucky to be a pal of Rod's.

Rod leaned into a pitch. Bat met ball solidly. Like a white bead shot from a gun the ball sailed in a high arc to deep center field. A yell burst from the crowd at the same time. Then it faded with disappoint-

ment as the ball came down inside the park and was caught.

Rod caught streaking grounders at second base. As the game went on he pulled off sparkling plays. One was an over-the-shoulder catch of a pop fly to short right field. He doubled, knocking in two runs, and then had bad luck when he hit into a double play.

Rod argued with the base umpire about the call at first, taking off his cap and whipping it hard against his thigh. He was angry — real angry about the call.

"There he goes," a fan behind Sandy remarked. "There goes his hot head again."

Sandy felt a shiver pierce through him, then thought: Rod won't argue long. He'll stop any second now and walk to the bench. But Rod didn't. He kept on arguing.

Suddenly the manager leaped out of the dugout and ran down the baseline toward first. "Rod!" he yelled. "Stop that and come here and sit down!"

"But I was safe!" Rod yelled back.

"Safe or not, get back here!" cried the manager. "You can't change his mind!"

"Good ballplayer, if it wasn't for his be-

91

ing a hothead," the fan said as Rod walked off the field.

"He's lucky," another said. "If the manager hadn't run out there, Temple would've been thrown out of the game."

The Redwings won 4 to 3. Rod had gotten two hits out of four times at bat. "I was robbed at first," he said to Sandy as they headed for home on the motor scooter. "That ump's as blind as a bat."

Sandy didn't say anything. But it looked to him as though the umpire had made a good call.

They reached a junction where a road turned left, heading toward Deerhead Lake. Rod maneuvered the bike onto it. The road dipped sharply and Rod sent the scooter blazing down it like a red bullet on wheels.

"Hang on!" yelled Rod. The wind

whipped against their faces, flapped their pant legs. It was the fastest ride that Sandy had ever had on the scooter. He hung on the handgrips as hard as he could.

Far ahead of them was a truck. It was going downhill in the same direction they were, but very slowly. Rod approached it and started to pass. They were almost abreast of it when Sandy saw, a short distance beyond them, a car coming around a curve!

Sandy sucked in his breath. What was Rod going to do? Try to pass the truck, or slow down and get behind it again?

Rod didn't do either. As the car came closer Rod swung to the *left* — off the road. Sandy closed his eyes tightly, knowing that he would never have done what Rod had done.

The scooter struck a rock on the side of the road, skidded into a two-cabled railing, and fell on its side, sending Rod and Sandy spilling over the ground.

11

SANDY rose to his feet. His right shoulder ached. It had taken most of the shock of his fall. He pulled up the sleeve of his sweater and saw the bruise on his elbow. It was bleeding a little. He pulled the sleeve down and looked at Rod Temple.

Rod was rising to his feet a couple of yards away. "You hurt?" he asked.

"Just an ache in my shoulder and a scratch on my elbow," said Sandy. "How about you?"

"That's about what I've got."

Rod brushed dirt off his uniform, picked up his cap, slapped it against his leg and put it on. Two men came running down the hill. Their car, the one Rod had driven off the road to avoid, was parked a short distance away.

"You boys hurt?" one of the men yelled.

"No, we're okay," said Rod.

"You sure?" asked the second man. "That looked like quite a spill."

"I'm sure."

"How about you?" the man asked Sandy. "You all right?"

Sandy nodded. "I'm okay."

The men shook their heads, as if the boys' not getting hurt was a miracle. They picked up the scooter and looked at it. It was badly scratched and the front wheel was twisted.

"I don't think you'll be able to ride this,"

observed the first man. "Look at that wheel."

"I'll leave it here and have someone pick it up later," said Rod. He took the scooter, looked over the damages, then set it against the cables. "It won't be much of a job to fix," he said. "Come on, Sandy. Let's start walking."

"Want us to drive you home?"

"No, thanks. We can walk. Let's go, Sandy."

The men shrugged, and Sandy stared at Rod. Why didn't he accept their invitation? There was still a long way to go. Was it because Rod was embarrassed for having gotten into that accident? Well, he wouldn't have if he had slowed down and stayed behind the truck.

They reached the bottom of the road, walking on the left-hand side, facing traffic. Five minutes later they reached the bridge and to the far right of it was the gorge. A path wound alongside the creek that led to the gorge. The boys crossed the bridge and Rod started to lead the way up the path.

"Come on," he said. "We'll take a short-cut up."

Sandy frowned. "A shortcut? How?"

Rod looked at him as if he were stupid. "How? We'll walk through the gorge and climb up it to the upper road, that's how. Otherwise we'd take a week getting home on this road."

"Then, why — why didn't you let those guys drive us home?" asked Sandy, puzzled.

"Just because, that's why," Rod snorted. "Think I want to listen to them tell me how I should drive my scooter? I knew I shouldn't have driven off the left side of the road like I did. But I did. And I would've been all right if I'd seen that lousy rock. But I didn't see it. Anyway, I don't want to talk about it. And don't you tell anybody about it, either, see?"

Sandy swallowed an ache in his throat. Rod had never talked like this to him before. He had never expected Rod to sound off like this. Not to Sandy, his friend. Suddenly Sandy wondered, *Am I really Rod's friend? Would he talk to me like that if I were?*

At that moment he wished he were anywhere else but here with Rod Temple.

The path wound alongside the creek and snaked around a bend. Layers of rock rose to enormous heights on both sides. Does Rod expect us to climb *that?* Sandy wondered.

Straight ahead, like a carpenter's long, silver pencil, Deerhead Falls glistened in the sunlight. A vapor spray looked like a steadily moving silk curtain at its bottom.

"Look!" said Sandy. "A rainbow!"

"I see it, I see it," grumbled Rod.

They walked within a hundred yards of the falls, then Rod looked up the steep, rocky bank at their left. "This looks the best place to climb," he said. "Let's go."

The bank was almost straight up, with trees and brush here and there to grab hold of and help them along. Sandy didn't think they could climb it, but he didn't say anything. Rod would only grumble at him again.

They started the climb. Sandy followed almost the exact steps Rod was taking, grabbing hold of the same brush and trees.

Gradually the path and the creek below sank farther and farther away. Maybe Rod was right, after all, Sandy admitted. Climbing the steep bank was easier than it looked.

"How you doing?" Rod asked when they were halfway up.

Sandy grinned. "Okay."

He held onto a tree stump and looked down. He got dizzy and shut his eyes. The path and the creek seemed a mile below them. He opened his eyes and promised himself not to look down again.

They climbed another twenty feet or so, and then Rod stepped onto a flat ledge that seemed big enough for both of them to stand on.

"Watch that nest," cautioned Rod. "Could be a hawk's, or an eagle's."

The large nest lay near the edge. Inside were broken pieces of eggshells. Sandy looked at their surroundings. Layers of rock curved out behind them like the side of a dish. A cold, prickly sensation came over him and he looked at Rod. Their eyes seemed to meet at the same time.

"We're stuck!" cried Rod. "We can't get out of here!"

Sandy backed against the wall, striking his head against a rock. "Can't — can't we go back down?"

"Oh, yeah? Take a look down there. Think you can climb back down *there?*"

Sandy looked over the edge and drew back. "No," he said. "What — what are we going to do, Rod?"

"Yell, that's what."

Rod began yelling. "He-lloooo, there! He-lloooo!"

He and Sandy alternated their yells. And then they yelled together. But minutes passed. Only Rod dared to look down through the long, empty space below them.

"No one hears us," he said softly. "There's no one down there."

He smacked a fist hard into the palm of his other hand. "Darn! I wouldn't mind it so much if you weren't with me. Another big kid and I . . . we'd figure this out. But you —" He stopped and struck a fist into his palm again. "A kid! What did I have to get mixed up with a *kid* for?"

The remark was like a hard slap on the face. Sandy's eyes blurred. "It — it's not my fault we're stuck up here," he said.

"Shut up!" shouted Rod. "Shut up! Hear me?" And then he blinked, took a deep breath, exhaled it. His eyes turned friendly.

He put an arm around Sandy's shoulders.

"Sorry, kid. I didn't mean it. Honest, I didn't. You're okay. Come on. Let's yell some more . . . together."

12

MOM *will be waiting for me and I'll be late. She won't be able to go to work till Pop comes home.*

Sandy looked at his watch. Five after six! Still there was no one below. No one who had heard their yells.

"He-lloooo!" Rod yelled again. "He-lloooo down there!"

Fifteen minutes passed. A half hour. And then Rod shouted, "Look! There's people down there! They're looking up! He-lloooo! He-elp us! We can't get do-own!"

Sandy, flat on his stomach, peered over the edge of the precipice. It was like watching a movie of tiny people. There were five of them. They were looking up! They had heard!

"We hear you!" a man shouted back. "We'll get you out of there!"

Rod slapped Sandy happily on the back. "They heard us!"

A couple of the men left. Fifteen minutes later — how the time dragged — more men appeared below. And then a voice reached them, loud and clear, and Sandy saw that the man was using a megaphone.

"Listen, boys! Someone will get down to you from above with a rope! Don't be frightened! You'll be all right!"

At last dirt and stones began falling

down around them. Someone was coming down!

"More to the left!" ordered the voice over the megaphone. "A little more! Okay!"

Moments later a man appeared over the ledge, a rope secured around his waist.

He was holding a second rope, the other end of which ran up the side of the gorge to the ground above.

"Hello!" he greeted. "How in the world did you get here?"

"Climbed up," said Rod. "Couldn't make it any further."

"Well, who wants to go first?"

"Take Sandy," said Rod.

"Okay. Get this rope under your armpits, son, and I'll tie it," said the rescuer. He helped Sandy, then put a hand to his mouth and yelled up. "Okay, Jim! Haul 'er up! Easy!"

The rope stiffened. Sandy stepped to the side of the dishlike ledge, then little by little was lifted to the flat plateau above. Three men met him. One was a policeman, the other two firemen of the Sharil Fire Department.

"Hello, son," one of the firemen said. "What's your name?"

"Sandy Varga."

"John Varga's son?"

Sandy nodded.

"Okay. Get into that car. Let's get the other boy, Jim."

Pop was home when Sandy got there. He looked furious. The policeman accompanied Sandy into the house and explained to Pop what had happened.

"Don't be harsh on him, Mr. Varga," he said. "The other boy, Rodney Temple, admitted that he was the one who had suggested taking a shortcut up the gorge. He took all the blame."

Pop took a casserole out of the oven and put it on the table for Sandy. It was almost eight o'clock. Then Pop telephoned Mom and told her that Sandy was home and everything else that had happened.

Afterwards Sandy lay on the lawn, keeping an eye on Jo Ann and Elizabeth. The terrifying experience of being on the ledge passed through his mind like a bad dream. Suppose that no one had showed up below? Would he and Rod have been able to sleep there throughout the night? Not me, thought Sandy. I would be awake all night. He shuddered and tried to drive the nightmarish thought out of his mind.

Then and there he promised himself that he would never ride with Rod Temple again. At least, not until he was bigger. He had been all wrong in thinking that he and Rod fitted like peas in a pod. Rod was too grown-up for him. His kind of fun was different than Sandy's. He took risks with his motor scooter. He lost his temper on the baseball diamond.

And to top it off he called me a kid! thought Sandy. I really don't mind that. It was the way he said it. As if *kid* was dirty. I'm sure Rod liked me a little or he wouldn't have taken me to the ball game, or on rides on his motor scooter. But he's a lot older than me. And different. Too different. We just don't *fit* together, that's all.

Just then Sandy caught sight of Nibbs Spry and Jules Anderson walking down the street. He dismissed Rod from his mind and sprang to his feet.

"Nibbs! Jules!" he shouted. "Hi, ya, guys!"

They looked. They waved. But kept on walking.

13

SANDY VARGA had never lived through such a lonesome weekend. He had seen Nibbs Spry and Jules Anderson in the street a few times, but at a distance. They didn't come over to his house as they used to. None of the other guys did, either.

They used to play catch in the back yard, play pool on the small pool table in the basement and talk about models. Nibbs was a model buff, too. He liked to assemble model ships. Jules enjoyed putting together models of great athletes —

Babe Ruth, Lou Gehrig, and many others. Ike Norman used to come over with his skateboard and take turns riding it with Sandy.

Everything was changed. You'd think that Sandy had moved out of Sharil. They had dropped him like a hot iron.

Well, whose fault was it, anyway? Hadn't he favored Rod Temple over them? Hadn't he wanted to be with Rod Temple and his motor scooter every chance he had?

Nibbs, Jules, Ike, all the others — they were his real friends. He had hurt them by favoring Rod over them. How could he tell them he had been all wrong?

Tuesday's game against the Ripcords came too soon. Sandy wished it would rain or that he'd get sick so he couldn't play.

The guys won't care whether I show up or not, he thought. But Coach Malone might care. He didn't know about Sandy's troubles.

The Spacemen had last raps and Sandy was at short.

"Nice to be the coach's pet," remarked Kerry.

Sandy's eyes flashed. "What do you mean by that crack?"

"Nobody except a pet could play three or four innings, then go home," answered Kerry.

So it was that, too! Not only his going around with Rod.

A Texas leaguer over first! Right fielder Stubby Tobin came in, fielded the ball, relayed it to second.

"Come on, Dick!" The infielders' chatter grew louder. "Let's get two!"

Third baseman Kerry Dean and first baseman Ken Bockman played in on the grass, expecting a bunt. It *was* a bunt! A neat one down the first-base line! But it was hit softly and Dick Regan fielded it. He whipped it to Sandy covering second. Out! Sandy pegged to first. A wild throw! The runner touched first, went on to second.

There was none of that "Forget it, Sandy! Get 'em the next time!" coming from the guys. Nibbs, his best friend, didn't say a word to him.

The next hitter swung at a low pitch. *Crack!* A hard grounder down to Sandy's left side. Sandy went after it, but he had started too late. He hadn't been ready. He

116

was thinking about Nibbs and the other guys, not about the game. The ball bounded to the outfield for a hit and the runner on second scored.

The next Ripcord blasted a pitch over second, scoring another run. A strikeout, and a pop fly, ended the top half of the inning.

Kerry Dean, batting against Stinky Hayes, the Ripcords' short right-hander, drew a walk on five pitches. Nibbs Spry fouled a pitch down the left-field line, then singled through the pitcher's box. The Ripcord center fielder hustled after the ball and kept Kerry on second. Sandy stepped to the plate.

He didn't feel well at all. He didn't care whether he hit the ball or not. Always before the whole bench would yell at him to "Wallop that apple, Sandy!" It was different now. Only two or three of the guys said anything.

The first pitch was a ball. He cut at the next one, popped it high into the air and trotted to first. He was halfway there when the first baseman caught it for the out.

Cookie Lamarr was up next. Coach Malone had made a slight change in the lineup. Cookie used to play the last two or three innings.

The pitch. Cookie swung. A slow grounder to short! Cookie dropped his bat and raced hard for first as the shortstop came in for the hop. He caught the ball, tossed it to third. Kerry was out! The third baseman pegged to first. Safe!

Two away. Marty Loomis came up and belted the third pitch for a double, scoring

Nibbs. Stubby flied out. The first inning was over.

Dick Regan's first pitch to the Ripcord leadoff man was so high that Marty Loomis couldn't reach it. The ball sailed to the backstop screen. Phil Peters ran over, picked it up and tossed it to the umpire. The umpire looked it over and tossed it to Dick.

"Play ball," he said.

Dick settled down and struck the Ripcord out. The next man blasted a double and the next walked.

"Get two!" shouted Kerry Dean at third.

A grass-cutting grounder to short! Sandy waited for the hop. The ball struck the thumb of his glove, bounced up against his chest and rolled in front of him. He stumbled backward, chased after the ball,

picked it up and heaved it. He didn't look directly at whom he was throwing. It was supposed to be to Ken Bockman at first. But the ball missed Ken by yards!

A run scored and the umpire held up the other runners on third and second.

Sandy spun disgustedly and slapped the glove against his thigh. What a stupid play that was!

Dick walked the next man, filling the bases. He sure looked nervous. He took off his cap, wiped his face, put his cap back on and climbed the mound. The infielders yelled, "Strike 'im out, Dick! Whiff 'im!"

Sandy didn't feel like yelling, but now and then he did. "Come on, boy! Come on!" he shouted.

Crack! A single over second! Two runs scored. Then a pop fly and a grounder back to Dick, and the top of the second inning was over.

Wish it was six-forty, thought Sandy. Phil was holding his wristwatch.

Ken started the bottom of the second with a hit between first and second base. The Ripcord infielder fumbled it and Ken

121

was safe at first. Then Punk Peters blasted one to left center for a double. Ken advanced to third. Dick fanned. Then Kerry singled through second and Ken scored. Punk ran all the way in, too, sliding into home on a close play. He was safe and Kerry stopped on second base.

Nibbs Spry flied out and Sandy, watching two strikes go by, swung at the third one and struck out.

Ripcords 5; Spacemen 3.

"What time is it, Phil?" Sandy asked.

Phil looked at the watch. "Almost six-fifteen." He looked at Sandy curiously. "What's the matter, Sandy? You're not playing good at all today."

Sandy trotted out to short without answering.

The Ripcords picked up another run. The Spacemen didn't. In the top of the fourth Sandy let a hot grounder go through his legs, then missed a high pop fly, accounting for two of the five runs the Ripcords scored that half-inning. He didn't remember when he had played a worse game.

The score was 11–3 when he left for home. He knew the guys were looking at him, but he said nothing. He saw in the Sharil *Journal* the next day that the final score was 13–8.

14

SANDY was glad for the long Fourth
of July weekend. The family rented
a cabin at Deerhead State Park from Saturday through Monday. Monday was the
Fourth. Pop had had the cabin reserved
for those three days since March.

Pop liked to fish and so did Pete and
Sandy. They caught nearly a dozen of
black bass and Mom cooked them for
supper.

You have to be quiet when you fish.
Talking will disturb the fish and they

won't bite. Pop was pretty strict about it. It was this quiet that Sandy didn't like. It left him with all the time in the world to think — and what he thought about were the guys, Nibbs Spry, Jules Anderson, Ike Norman, and the others.

At night he dreamed about them, too. But their faces seemed to be hidden in shadows from which they refused to appear. It was awful.

He thought about Rod Temple, too. Rod had seemed so nice at times, but he never was a real friend. Sandy hadn't minded paying Rod's way at the miniature golf course, or buying Rod a cone of ice cream. Rod had given him rides on the motor scooter to more than make up for those favors. It just had seemed funny that every time Rod had stopped to buy something he'd discover that he had left his wallet home. Yet he wouldn't have dared to drive without his license, would he? Wouldn't he be carrying that in a wallet?

Stopping at the girls' softball game that afternoon was another example. Rod had been gone so long he seemed to have forgotten that he had left Sandy with his scooter. A friend — a *real* friend — wouldn't have done that.

Maybe it wasn't all Rod's fault. Maybe his parents were to blame more than Rod was. Their arguments could make a household miserable to live in.

Rod was unhappy, no doubt about that. And at times he got bitter, like the time he had shouted at Sandy when they were trapped on the side of the gorge. Maybe it was doing things like that that kept him from having friends. Friends his own age.

Guess being popular didn't mean a guy had friends, too.

But it was my fault that I'd lost my friends, thought Sandy. I had ignored them. I had pretended I was a hotshot because I was with Rod. And I'm ashamed to tell them that I leave the games early because I have to watch my kid sisters.

How was he going to get them back? How was he going to fix things so that they'd all be like they were before?

He didn't know what to do, but he had to do *something*.

He still hadn't solved the problem by the time they had left for home Monday night. Dad wanted to get home early, to have a good night's sleep and be fresh for work in the morning.

Sandy wished Tuesday would never come. The Spacemen were playing the

Batwings. Though the Spacemen had beat them before, the Batwings were no pushovers.

It wasn't winning or losing that really bothered him. It was facing the guys — especially Nibbs and Jules. As long as he could remember they were his closest friends. Now he and they were miles apart. He had never realized before how lonely it was not to have at least one friend — a friend your age — who you could call up on the phone, or yell at on the street, or whose house to go to and spend a few hours. You might as well have never been born.

The Spacemen had first raps and Kerry Dean led off with a pop fly to the first baseman. Nibbs waited out Ed Thomas, the Batwings' short right-hander. Then, with a two-and-two count, he rapped a hit just over Ed's head. Ed leaped, but not high enough. Nibbs was on with a single.

Sandy came up. He tapped the tip of his bat against the plate and looked at Nibbs standing with his hands on his knees on first. None of that "Come on, Sandy! Blast it!" from Nibbs as there used to be. Nibbs was dead silent. From the bench came a few scattered yells. And from the stands. It seemed that only a few cared whether he hit or not.

Crack! A pop fly straight up into the air over his head. He dropped his bat, started to run. Nibbs had run off the bag, was standing several feet away from it, watching a Batwing go after the ball. It was either the catcher or the pitcher, Sandy didn't look to see.

Then the Batwing fans let out a happy yell and Nibbs hurried back to first. Sandy turned two-thirds of the way to the base and jogged back to the dugout, in time to see the catcher toss the ball to the third baseman.

"Get one the next time, Sandy," a fan said.

Well, at least someone was rooting for him.

Cookie Lamarr smashed a long shallow drive between left and center fields, scoring Nibbs, and stopped on third for a neat triple. Marty Loomis struck out to end the top of the first inning.

Duke Miller struck out the first Batwing hitter and the second hit a slow grounder to him which he fielded easily. The next batter popped a blooping fly to him. It was Duke all the way that bottom half of the inning.

Stubby got on due to an error by the

third baseman, then went to second on Ken Bockman's sacrifice bunt. Punk Peters singled and Duke pounded a double, scoring Stubby. Ike Norman held Punk up at third.

"Ducks on the pond!" yelled a fan. "Knock 'em in!"

Kerry flied out for the second time. Then Nibbs walked, loading the bases, and Sandy came to bat.

"Sandy, put on your helmet," said the umpire.

Sandy flushed. He had forgotten his protective helmet! He turned and started to get one, but Phil was bringing it to him.

"Thanks, Phil," he said softly.

He put the helmet on and stepped into the box. Sweat popped out on his forehead. He held his bat over his shoulder, waving it back and forth just a little, and watched Ed Thomas stretch and throw. The pitch looked letter-high. He swung.

"Strike one!" yelled the ump.

"Thataway to pitch, Eddie!" cried the Batwing fans.

"Hit that ol' onion!" shouted the Spacemen rooters.

Another pitch almost in the same spot. Sandy swung.

"Strike two!"

Sandy grit his teeth. Sweat blurred his eyes and he wiped it away. He got ready for Ed's next pitch. It was in there again and he swung.

"Strike three!"

A roar burst from the Batwing fans and players. Sandy, his heart a ball of lead, tossed bat and helmet toward the dugout and trotted out to short, his eyes lowered to the grass at his feet.

The first ball Duke pitched was knocked to Sandy. Still flustered over the strikeout with the bases loaded, Sandy fumbled it. Finally he picked it up. By then it was too late to throw.

The next Batwing hit to Nibbs. Nibbs caught the grounder, turned to toss the ball to Sandy at second. *But Sandy wasn't there!*

Sandy woke up. He had forgotten about a possible double play! He rushed to second. Again he was too late. He caught Nibbs's throw, but the runner was already there. Hurriedly he pegged to first. The peg was wild. Both runners advanced a base.

The Batwings kept hitting and knocked in three runs before the Spacemen could get them out. The Spacemen picked up three, including a homer by Ken Bockman. But the Batwings scored four runs in the bottom of the third — two on Sandy's two errors — and climbed into the lead, 7 to 5.

When the Spacemen came to bat it was almost time for Sandy to leave for home. He was first batter, and he was greatly relieved when Coach Malone had Ike Norman pinch-hit for him. He watched Ike drop a single over second base. Then, his glove on his hand, trotted all the way home.

His eyes popped at sight of Mom. She and Pop were sitting on lawn chairs in the back yard, watching Jo Ann and Elizabeth playing with the dollhouse.

Sandy stared. "Mom! Aren't you going to work?"

She smiled. "I told you this morning. I have vacation all this week."

15

SANDY didn't go back to the game. He didn't care to show himself there again today, not after those errors he had made.

They were silly errors. He would not have made them if he had kept his mind on what he was doing. Like throwing that wild peg to first base, for instance. If he had been thinking he would've realized that the runner was going to be safe.

He read the final score in Wednesday's Sharil *Journal*. The Batwings had won 9 to 8.

"Sandor," Mom said early that after-noon, "Nibbs and your other friends have not been here in a long time. Is there something wrong?"

He blushed. "They're sore at me."

Her eyes widened. "Sore? Why?"

"Well, quite a few times I went with Rod Temple on his scooter instead of with them. I didn't realize I was ignoring them. Guess I thought Rod and I were . . . well, hotshots. And they don't like my leaving the game after I play three or four innings."

"Do they know you must come home to watch over your sisters?"

"No. I haven't told them."

"Then you should. It is nothing to be ashamed of. And on the baseball field be friendly to them as you were before.

Maybe they think you are still a — a hot-shot, and don't want to talk to *them*."

Sandy thought about it. "Maybe you're right, Mom. Maybe that's what they think. I can try, anyway."

Mom patted his hand. "Since I don't work this week, I will go to your ball game and take Jo Ann and Elizabeth with me. We will all cheer for you."

The Sharks had first raps against the Spacemen on Thursday. Mom sat with Jo Ann and Elizabeth behind the back-stop screen. Sandy wished Pop was there, too. Pop hadn't seen a game this year. But he was working.

It was hard to start shouting in the in-field, shouting the way he used to before things had happened between him and his friends. But he tried. "Come on, Dick! Drill that pill by 'im!"

Kerry Dean kept up the chatter too. Then Nibbs, Ken and Marty. Cookie Lamarr, Stubby Tobin and Punk Peters joined in from the outfield.

Dick pitched hard. A grounder to Kerry, a pop-up to Sandy, a strikeout. The Sharks went down one, two, three.

Kerry Dean led off with a walk. Nibbs struck out.

"Okay, Nibbs!" shouted Sandy. "Hit him next time!"

It was hard yelling that. But he forced himself to, and Nibbs looked at him with a kind of startled expression on his face.

Sandy pulled on a helmet and walked to the plate. He wondered if Nibbs, Jules or Punk would yell something at him, but none of them did. It was the same few other guys who yelled.

He waited out Red Billings's pitches, got a two-two count, then swung at a knee-high pitch. A long fly to center. The Sharks' center fielder raced back and caught it. Cookie, up next, drilled a grass-cutter over the third-base sack for two bases, driving in Kerry. The shortstop missed Marty's hard grounder, and Cookie advanced to third. Stubby Tobin flied out to end the bottom half of the first inning.

Dick Regan's first pitch was drilled hard down to short. Sandy, holding his breath, waited for it. He tried to play the hop — missed! The ball bounded over his head and rolled to the edge of the grass behind him. He raced after it, picked it up, started to throw, saw that it was too late and held up.

"Sorry, Dick," he said as he tossed Dick the ball.

"Forget it," said Dick. "Get two."

Sandy started the chatter. He wasn't going to let that error bother him. His teammates quickly joined in. Dick threw. A long drive to left center! Sandy took the throw-in from Cookie, relayed it home. It was a long triple, scoring a run.

Then Nibbs missed a hot grounder, and the man on third scored. Nibbs was scowling.

"Forget it, Nibbs!" yelled Sandy. "Let's get two!"

Nibbs looked at him. A smile broke across his face. Sandy smiled back.

Nibbs spat into his glove. "C'mon!" he shouted. "Let's go!"

A blistering grounder to second. Sandy

ran over to cover. Nibbs fielded the ball, tossed it to Sandy. Sandy caught it, touched the bag, pegged to first. A double play!

The Spacemen got a hit in the bottom of the second, but failed to score. In the top of the third the Sharks couldn't score, either. Sandy started off the bottom of the inning with a double. Cookie singled. Sandy ran as hard as he could around third and slid into home under the Sharks' catcher's mitt. Safe!

"Nice run, Sandy!" cried Kerry. "Hey, isn't it almost time you left for home?"

"I don't have to watch my kid sisters to-day." Sandy grinned, pointing at the stands. "They're here with my mother. She doesn't have to work today."

Kerry, and some of the other guys who

heard him, stared. "Is that why you always quit so early?"

"Sure. What other reason would there be?"

He expected a laugh. But they just looked at him, sort of dumbfounded.

Red Billings began to act shaken up. He walked Marty, then struck out Stubby. That didn't dim the Spacemen's hopes, though. Keeping up their steady chatter, they sounded like a chorus. It was like it used to be. Only better. Much better.

"Blast it, Ken!" they shouted as Ken Bockman stepped to the plate. "Out of the park!"

Ken almost did. The long blast to right center went for three bases, scoring Cookie and Marty. Punk flied out. The shortstop missed Dick's sizzling grounder and Ken scored. Kerry flied out to end the big half-inning.

The Sharks picked up two in the top of the fourth. The Spacemen got them back on a double by Nibbs, a single by Sandy, and an error. The Sharks hit Dick Regan hard in the fifth, collecting two runs. Two men were on when Coach Malone took Dick out and put in Duke Miller.

Duke seemed to have trouble getting

the ball over the plate. He walked the batter. A scratch single drove in the Sharks' third run of the inning. Then Duke bore down, and, with the help of his teammates, retired the Sharks.

Duke led off in the bottom of the fifth. A cheer greeted him as he strode to the plate. *Crack!* A high-hopping grounder over Red's head for a single. Then Frank Mintz, who had taken Kerry's place at third, lined one out to deep left. It kept going . . . going . . . It was gone! A home run!

Nibbs singled, then was put out when Ike Norman hit into a double play. Jules ended the top half of the inning by flying out.

The Sharks came up for their last try to go ahead again. The Spacemen were leading 9 to 7. A strikeout by Duke, a fly ball to Oink Decker in right field, and a grounder to Nibbs ended the ball game.

" 'A way to pitch!" yelled Sandy as he rushed out to Duke and grabbed his hand. "Nice going, Nibbs! Looked as if you had a magnetic glove!"

Nibbs laughed. "How about going swimming after we get out of these monkey suits?"

"Sure!" exclaimed Sandy. "How about it, Jules?"

"Swimming? Man, I'm pooped! But, sure! Why not?"

They started off the field together.

"Sandor! Wait for us!" came a cry behind them.

Sandy looked over his shoulder. There were Mom and his two sisters running after him, all three smiling happily.